I celebrated World Book Day 2021 with this gift from my local bookseller and Hachette Children's Group

#ShareAStory

THE PLANET OMAR SERIES

ACCIDENTAL TROUBLE MAGNET

UNEXPECTED SUPER SPY

INCREDIBLE RESCUE MISSION

WORLD BOOK DAY

WORLD BOOK DAY'S mission is to offer every child and young person the opportunity to read and love books by giving you the chance to have a book of your own.

To find out more, and for loads of fun activities and recommendations to help you keep reading visit worldbookday.com

WORLD BOOK DAY is a charity funded by publishers and booksellers in the UK and Ireland.

WORLD BOOK DAY is also made possible by generous sponsorship from National Book Tokens and support from authors and illustrators.

HODDER CHILDREN'S BOOKS

First published in Great Britain in 2021 by Hodder & Stoughton

1 3 5 7 9 10 8 6 4 2

Text copyright © Zanib Mian, 2021
Illustrations by Nasaya Mafaridik and Kyan Cheng.
Illustrations copyright © Hodder & Stoughton Limited, 2021

A CIP catalogue record for this book
is available from the British Library.

ISBN 978 1 444 95994 9
Export ISBN 978 1 444 95993 2

Printed and bound in Great Britain by
Clays Ltd, Elcograf S.p.A

The paper and board used in this book
are made from wood from responsible sources.

Hodder Children's Books
An imprint of
Hachette Children's Group
Part of Hodder & Stoughton
Carmelite House
50 Victoria Embankment
London, EC4Y 0DZ

An Hachette UK Company
www.hachette.co.uk

www.hachettechildrens.co.uk

ZANIB MIAN

PLANET OMAR

OPERATION KIND

ILLUSTRATED BY NASAYA MAFARIDIK AND KYAN CHENG

HODDER

ME

my name is Omar — this is my face

I have a (HUGE) imagination

I once tried to drink hanging upside down, but the juice went up my nose

I will do anything for my friends

DANIEL AND SUZY

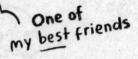

One of
my **best** friends

Crazy
but cool

Brother
and sister

Loves books

Has to go to the
hospital a lot

CHARLIE

also my
best friend

toothy grin
extraordinaire

has a really
funny grandma

can write with
both hands

MUM AND DAD

nerdy scientists

CHAPTER 1

'EwwwwwWwww!'

That was me complaining about the sight I was seeing.

Daniel had stuck two After Eight chocolate wrappers up his nose. One in each nostril.

'The wrappers just smell so **yummy** that I had to do it – I want to smell them for ages!' he explained, as if it was the most normal thing to do if you thought something smelt **NICE**.

'I like the smell of strawberries, but you don't see me walking around with them up my nose,' I said.

'That's only because they wouldn't fit.'

That made me **EXPLODE WITH LAUGHTER**. Sometimes Daniel can be so ridiculous.

We got back to what we were supposed to be doing, which was searching online for

1

someone selling a signed
copy of a book by Angelina
Kind.

We were at my house, in
my room, on my bed. I like imagining zooming
into us like that, like Google Earth does when
you look at your house. I pictured us
from even further away. We were
in the Milky Way galaxy, on Earth,
in Europe, in the UK, in England, in London,
at my house, in my room, on my bed ... cool!

Daniel was at my house this **weekend**,
because his parents had to go to the hospital
again, to take care of his little sister, Suzy,
who was having another operation. He was
feeling really sorry for her and wanted to do
something that would make her light up so
bright the sun would be jealous. That's how
he explained it. And since Angelina Kind was
Suzy's most **favourite** author
EVER, Daniel thought a signed book would be
just the thing.

Angelina Kind is Canadian and she's written famous books that have been made into movies that we've all seen. She seems really **NICE** too, but that could just be because of her name. Before her, I didn't even know Kind could be a surname. It made me wonder what my name would be if it was an adjective.

'You would be Daniel Hilarious,' I told Daniel.

'You would be **OMAR SUPER.**'

'What? Why?'

'Because you say it **A LOT.**'

'I super do not.' I grinned. Suddenly, Daniel jumped off the bed, shrieking, 'She's here! In the UK! Angelina Kind is here! She's doing a book-signing thing in Scotland.'

'Woah! That means you can get a book signed with Suzy's actual name in it and maybe a message too,' I said, *excited*.

'Exactlyyyyyyyy!' said Daniel, doing forward rolls all over my carpet, as if he had to use up his excited energy.

'But Scotland is **super** far,' I pointed out.

Daniel sat still, worried now, and said, 'Does that mean we can't go?'

I looked at the laptop screen.

'Daniel, this is today. Her event is today only, from 6 to 8 p.m.'

We're going to miss it!' cried Daniel. And he lay down with his face smushed into the carpet.

I **didn't** like seeing my friend go from such springy excitement to motionless disappointment. Sometimes when I'm sad or disappointed, I imagine my dragon, *H2O*, swooping down from the clouds to cheer me up. Right now, I wished he was real, and not only in my *imagination*. He would have been able to take us to Scotland in minutes! (I'm hoping Allah will give me something like H_2O in heaven. I'm sure He will.)

Well, after H_2O, I guessed the PEANUT (our 4x4 car with a huge roaring, beasty engine) was the next best thing.

'Let's ask my mum and dad.' I poked the unmoving body on my carpet. '**COME ON.**'

We ran down the stairs and into the living room.

'Dad!' I panted. 'How long does it take to get to Scotland? Can you take us? Do you think the PEANUT can go as fast as a **dragon?**'

'Slow down.' Dad laughed. 'Why are we going to Scotland in such a panic?'

5

'Angelina Kind is there, signing books, but only today. Suzy absolutely L♡VES her and I really, realllllllllly want to get her a book with a message in it. It would make her feel so much better!' said Daniel, both fists clenched.

'It would be a mad dash ...' said Dad.

'Do it, darling!' said Mum, to my surprise. 'It's worth it if it's going to make Suzy happy.' And she looked at Dad with sparkly eyes.

'Jarvis. Prepare my suit for a cross-country mission,' said Dad, pretending to call out to his butler and flexing his muscles.

We all giggled.

'Can I go, too?' said Maryam, who had followed us down the stairs to see what the fuss was about. 'You might need my help.'

'Or because you're **obsessed** with Angelina Kind?' I said, trying my best to raise just one eyebrow at her, which I can never manage.

'She's all right ...' lied Maryam.

'Fine.' I shrugged. 'As long as you're not annoying.'

'I am **NEVER** annoying.'

'But what about Charlie? If Maryam's going, Charlie should go too, or he'll be sad we all went without him,' I said.

'Yeah!' said Daniel.

'OK, it's 9:30 a.m. now, we need to set off ASAP, so if his parents agree, we'll pick him up on the way,' said Dad. 'But doing the maths, I'm thinking it would be quickest to catch a train.'

We ran off to call Charlie, as Mum dialled Daniel's parents to check with them.

CHAPTER 2

Charlie took ages to answer. We put it on speakerphone.

'What are you doing today?' Daniel asked **'Ermmm**excitedly.

well, Mum and Dad are out so Nan is here to "babysit" me and ... well ... why?' He sounded distracted.

'We're all going to Scotland today, to meet **'WHAAAAAT?'**Angelina Kind.'

Now we had his attention!

'Yeah, so find out if you can go. We are leaving **SUPER** soon,' I said.

'I ... I ...' said Charlie, 'I can't ask Nan ...'

'Why not?' I asked.

'Arggghh!'

Charlie wailed on the line.

Daniel and I looked at each other, puzzled.

Finally, Charlie got his words together for us. 'Nan bought me this SCIENCE set, but she said I wasn't allowed to start using it until Mum or Dad was supervising me. But the thing is, I used it. And it went wrong and stained my hands red all over, and a little bit of my face too ... so now if I go downstairs, Nan will know I used it!'

Daniel and I rolled around laughing at the thought of Charlie being caught red-handed. What a mess.

HA

HA

HA

HA

HA

'Just ask her,' I breathed through my giggles.

'But she thinks I'm an *angel* and she calls me buttercup and honey blossom and I've never disappointed her in my life ...'

Buttercup and honey blossom just got me and Daniel laughing even more.

'If I go downstairs, she won't ever be able to look at me the same way again,' continued Charlie, clearly upset.

That made me feel BAD for laughing.

'I really want to go,' said Charlie, 'but doing something to upset Nan is my worst fear EVER!'

We calmed Charlie down by telling him that his nan OBVIOUSLY loved him so much she would forgive him if he said sorry. Eventually, he said he would do it because the only other way to hide this from his nan for the rest of the day was to get into bed with the covers over him and pretend he was sick, which would be the most boring day ever.

'Do it,' said Daniel. 'We'll come to pick you up really soon.'

Next, we ran around flinging things to take with us in our rucksacks.

By 10 a.m. Dad was ready to go, and so were we. He had decided that if we were going to have a real chance of getting there **On time,** we weren't going to take the PEANUT all the way to Scotland. We were going to get a lift to Euston station and catch a train from there. Trains are even faster than beasty-engine cars.

But because so many of us needed to get to the station, we couldn't all fit in the PEANUT, so our lovely next-door neighbour, **Mrs Rogers,** was going to help Mum drop us off.

The only problem now was Esa, my **little brother,** who had been crying the whole time we were getting ready about wanting to go wherever Dad was going.

'We can't go, but we'll do something **fun** at home, just me and you, Esa,' Mum had said. But he was super cross and had made

that very clear by turning one of Mum's pot plants upside down.

We had finally got him to settle down on the sofa to watch cartoons when Mrs Rogers rang the doorbell, dressed without fail in one of her old lady cardigans and a

CHEEKY GRIN

which meant she had surprises to spring on us.

'We'll buy the tickets at the station. We've got plenty of time to do that and catch the train at noon,' said Dad, as he rummaged around in the drawer for the keys to the PEANUT. 'Darling, where are the car keys?'

'In the drawer. They're <u>ALWAYS</u> in the drawer.' Mum answered.

she checked too while Dad patted all the pockets he had.

'Maybe they're in one of your other jackets?' suggested Mum.

Dad sprinted up the stairs to go and check while we looked in ALL the places where the keys could possibly be. On the coffee table, in the kitchen, under the sofa – even in the washing machine. We couldn't find them.

Mrs Rogers sat on the sofa with Esa while she waited.

'Where on earth *are* they?' said Dad, puzzled, running his hands through his hair. 'We're going to be late!'

I imagined that the trolls I had been

reading about in Angelina Kind's book had come to life, peeled themselves off the pages and were hiding the keys for laughs. They would still be all flat and 2D because they were from a book, so it would be easy for them to hide, even though they were

BIG FAT trolls.

'John once lost his car keys, and it took him **three** days to finally find them in the kitty litter,' said Mrs Rogers, who often talks about her son, John. Then, pulling a little box from her bag, she asked, 'Would you like

some raisins, Esa?'

'Yes!' said Esa,
happily holding out his
hand.

Mrs Rogers poured some
into his palm and watched
as my clumsy little
brother dropped them all
straight away. He jumped off
the sofa to collect his raisins from the floor
and I couldn't believe what I saw: Esa had
been **sitting** on the keys!

I made a dash for them.

MUUUUUM! ESA HAD
THE KEYS!' I shouted.

Mum and Dad didn't know whether to
laugh or cry about the fact that a three year
old had outsmarted two scientists, a wise old
lady, and us older kids. He had been hiding
them that WHOLE time!

CHAPTER 3

It was 11:15 a.m. by the time we got into the car.

'I doubt we can make it for the 12 o'clock train now, but *I'll* drive!' Dad said, which was code for: *we have to get there* FASt!

'Oh, honey,' Mum said, handing over the keys, 'Mrs Rogers won't be able to keep up with you, anyway.'

Mrs Rogers and Dad exchanged a Secret smile and a wink at this.

Mum, Esa and Maryam got into the PEANUT with Dad, while Daniel and I jumped into Mrs Rogers' car.

Dad's engine scared away some birds as he started it with a roar. Daniel gave me a look that said: *yep, she won't be able to keep up with that.*

But when Dad sped off, switching lanes to get through traffic faster, Mrs Rogers was so close behind him that Daniel and I went completely nuts.

WOOOOOAAAAHH!

'Mrs Rogers, where did you learn to drive like that?' I asked.

'There's lots you don't know about me yet, Omar.' She chuckled, clearly enjoying every minute.

Didn't I tell you she's always full of surprises?

We got to Charlie's house. I bounced up to it and rang the doorbell.

Charlie came to the door. He had red ink all over his hands and a big blotch on his chin.

'Hello, buttercup,' I said.

'Hello!' Charlie grinned, not seeming to care that I was teasing him. He waved goodbye to his nan, and told us what  happened with her on our way to the station.

'She said she was my nan for ever, no matter what I did.' Charlie *beamed*. 'I didn't need to be scared at all.'

'Does that mean you can get away with anything at all? Because if it does, can we swap nans?' asked Daniel.

'No,' giggled Charlie. 'It was only because I was already very sorry. She said walking around with a red chin in public was punishment enough.'

'You do look really **silly**.' Daniel laughed.

'HEY!' said Charlie, covering his chin and falling on to me because Mrs Rogers took a sharp turn to keep on Dad's tail.

Just then, we heard a police car. Mrs Rogers pulled in to let it pass. We saw Dad pull in too, but instead of going past, the police car stopped by the PEANUT.

'UH-OH!' we all said, eyes

LIKE SAUCERS.

We jumped out and ran up to the car to see. I didn't say anything. There was a ROCK in my throat. I was really scared about Dad being in TROUBLE. Mum is always telling him he drives too fast.

'Is this your vehicle?' a police officer was saying.

Another officer was still
sitting in the car.

'Yes, it's mine,' said Dad
calmly. He gave me a
Smile. It was to tell
me everything was
going to be all right.

I was hoping
angels were
protecting Dad from
anything bad happening. They would
be if he said the dua (a prayer) for

leaving the house,

like he normally does. Angels are one thing
I have trouble imagining. I know that the
pictures in my head aren't as *awesome*
as the angels I read about in my books.
Apparently, Angel Gabriel has *600* wings!

The officer poked at a device in his hands.

'When did you buy it?'

'Oh, a few years ago. What year was it,
honey?' Dad asked Mum.

'2017,' said Mum.

'Hmmmm,' came the police officer's response. He didn't seem to believe Dad and just stared at his device.

'This isn't about the driving. They think the car is ' whispered Daniel to me and Charlie.

We watched on, frozen, as the second police officer got out of the car to join his partner.

'WHAT'S GOING ON?' asked the second officer.

'The vehicle's registered to a Miss Craig,' said the first officer.

'Let's have a look.' The second officer took the device. 'You've put the plates in wrong, you numpty! It's PE14 NUT, not NUY!'

The first officer looked like he had farted in front of the queen.

'Apologies for wasting your time, sir.' The second officer nodded at Dad.

'Have a good day now,' the embarrassed officer said, with red cheeks. I felt sorry for him. Maybe it was his first day? Maybe he needed glasses?

We all looked at each other, giggling at what had just happened. That turned from scary to funny SUPER quick!

'Hey, Dad. How did you know Mrs Rogers would be able to keep up with you?' I asked.

Dad chuckled. 'I've been a passenger in her car recently.'

'Well, no more of that silly driving, please,' said Mum. 'You're just lucky that wasn't about your lane hopping.'

We drove to the station more carefully the rest of the way. We said our goodbyes and we flew towards the station entrance, but by the time we got there, we had **missed** the train.

CHAPTER 4

It was 12:15 p.m.

Dad was <u>STILL</u> confident. He said that we could catch the 1 p.m train instead.

People stared at us as we walked towards the ticket booth, I guessed because of Charlie's bright red chin. And because Daniel insisted on speed walking. And because **Maryam** insisted on Instagramming everything as she walked, which meant she didn't look up from her phone.

'Are these all your children?' said the **LADY** at the ticket booth. She tucked her chin into her chest and stared at us over the rim of the glasses, instead of through them, making us all feel uncomfortable.

'No, no. These two are mine, and these are friends,' said Dad.

'HMMMMM. And what happened to this one's chin?' said the lady, moving her glasses down her nose to look at Charlie even harder over the rims.

'Does she even need those glasses?' whispered Daniel.

'My **science** experiment went wrong,' piped up Charlie, which surprised us as he's normally the shyest of all of us.

'Well, I might have to see proof that you are allowed to travel with these children,' said the lady in a

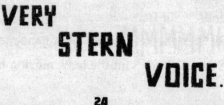

'That's reasonable,' said Dad, sheepishly rubbing the back of his head. 'And I could arrange that, but it's just that we've already missed one train and we're actually—'

Dad didn't get to finish his sentence, because Daniel pushed forward, wagging a **fingeR,** saying, 'Now you listen here ...' he peered at her name tag, '... Miranda! My little sister is a very sick girl in hospital and I'm her big brother and I'm going to  Scotland to get a signed book by Angelina Kind, and I can't think of anything else that will cheer her up, and we already might not make it on time, so listen you, just listen Miranda, give us those tickets and stop making my sister cry!'

Dad, Maryam, Charlie and I all watched in horror,

our jaws dropping at the scene Daniel was making. *She's going to call security*, my brain was screaming, *and then we will never get to go!*

But to our surprise, Miranda broke into a warm, *Sunshine* smile, placed her hand on her heart and took her glasses off completely.

'That's the most wonderful thing I've ever heard, in my twenty-three years working here,' she said. 'Why didn't you say you were on such an

IMPORTANT
MISSION?

I looked at Dad, and Dad looked at me, with a look that said: *yep, I don't understand this lady either!*

'I'll upgrade you to first class for this *extra special trip,*' Miranda was saying, tapping away at her keyboard.

'Wow, thank you very much,' said Dad.

Daniel's eyes
and skin went all
twinkly. I imagined
he was made of
stars, and if I popped him,
we would have a

BURST of stars all around

us ... But then there'd be no Daniel, I guess,
so that wouldn't be good.

'Can I take a picture of you for my social
media story please, Miranda?'

Maryam was still making this all about her,
but Miranda found this very flattering and
quickly posed with a huge smile.

Before we knew it, we were in big, cosy
first-class seats on the train, on time, ready to
set off. Everything was finally going well.

Or so we thought.

CHAPTER 5

We chatted away about our favourite Angelina Kind books, arguing over which was the **best** one, while we waited for the train to fill up and set off.

'I wonder who's going to sit there,' said Maryam, pointing at the one free seat in our area.

'What if it was Angelina Kind?' said Daniel, slapping his knee.

'Isn't she already in Scotland?' said Charlie.

'What if it's still someone **really cool,** like an astronaut?' I said.

'Or someone really, really stinky?' said Maryam. She **always** thinks of the worst things.

'Then you will have to sit next to him, because you said it!' said Daniel.

Then Charlie noticed someone approaching and said under his breath, 'Omar, what are the two animals you are most afraid of?'

'Pigeons and dogs,' I said.

'Well, I'm sorry, but it looks like the seat belongs to ...' and he just trailed off, letting us all turn our heads around to see for ourselves.

It was a blind man with a guide dog.

YIKES! I was going to have to spend almost five hours sitting next to a dog? My heart found its way into my throat.

'It's OK, Omar,' said Dad. 'Guide dogs are the nicest dogs imaginable.'

'Not for me. I can imagine dogs even nicer – like *without* ,'

I said, watching the blind man walking slowly to his seat with the help of another lady.

The dog was black, and a black dog is the **WHOLE** reason I have been scared of dogs since I was seven, because I got chased around the park by one. It didn't bite me, and the owner said it was just trying to play, but it was TERRIFYING. It **DEFINITELY** wanted me for its dinner.

I stood up, shaking, 'I don't think I can go any more, Dad ...'

I didn't want to leave our mission, but what if it jumped on me? What if it showed me its **TEETH**? What if it ATE me?

'It's not going to eat you,' said Daniel, as

if he read my thoughts, which was kind of weird. He looked at me with puppy dog eyes of his own. **'Are you going home?'**

Dad didn't say anything, but he came and put his arm round me.

'No ... I want to help you and Suzy. But can I sit on the furthest seat?' **I GULPED,** trying to swallow my fear, which was still this huge lump in my throat and bouncy balls in my heart.

The blind man was now at his seat
and he had heard what I said.

'DON'T WORRY, YOUNG MAN.

My name is Ranjit, and this is Steve. He's
won prizes for how gentle and
smart he is.'

Steve? That made
me giggle. It was such
a funny name for a dog.
Have you ever noticed that
once you can **LAUGH out loud**
at something, you don't feel as **panicky**
as you were before? I relaxed a teensy tiny bit
and sat down.

As I kept a close eye on Steve, the train
SET OFF.

We had a four hour and fifty minute
journey ahead of us, which
meant we would arrive
at Glasgow station in

Scotland around 6 p.m. and catch a cab to the
bookshop where Angelina Kind would be.

I wondered what we were going to do
for all those hours (apart from trying
not to get eaten by Steve). I passed
some time by looking out of the window,
and imagining that I wasn't on a train,

i WAS ACTUALLY ON A HOVERBOARD

swooping past all the fields and houses, and
then I had to stop imagining to check what
Steve was doing. He was sitting obediently by
his owner, and he didn't *look* like he wanted
to eat me.

'Hey, guys!' said Charlie suddenly.

'Yes, honey blossom?' said Daniel, giggling.

'Miranda said we were on a special mission, and we are! Let's give it a name, like that time we were searching for Mrs Hutchinson for **OpeRation MoOn Dust.'**

'How about Operation Kind?' I said.

'Very smart,' said Maryam.

'Nice double meaning.' Dad smiled.

I noticed that Ranjit had started patting the area around his seat. Steve stood up right away, picked up the walking stick in his jaws and passed it to him.

'**GOOD BOY**,' said Ranjit, and he started walking down the aisle. Steve was quickly in front of him. Daniel's bag was on the floor, and Steve

moved it over with his nose so that Ranjit
wouldn't trip over.

'Wow, that's **really cool**.' I said.

'It is,' said Charlie. 'Are you
still scared of him?'

'I think maybe he's **OK**.'
I grinned.

When Ranjit came back, with
Steve leading the way, we asked if
we could pet him. Charlie and Maryam
stroked him first. Steve stood very still and
didn't move away from Ranjit for a second.

'Want to try?' asked Dad.

I did. And when I patted him carefully on
his back, he wagged his
tail happily.

'Ah, he likes you,' said
Ranjit.

That made me feel

very proud

and happy. I didn't have
to keep an eye on Steve

after that, and even fell asleep for a bit on my seat.

I was only woken up by Daniel's loud,

‘NOOOOOOO!’

CHAPTER 6

The train had pulled to a stop but we were still in the *middle* of the countryside.

'Is it broken?' said Daniel in despair.

'Don't worry, they'll let us know what's happening,' said Dad.

'I bet it is broken, that's exactly the kind of luck we are having today,' Maryam moaned.

'Maybe the driver needed to stop for a wee,' said Charlie.

Just then, there was the *strangest* announcement I've ever heard.

There was a herd of sheep on the train tracks up ahead!

'For the love of **FLYiNG FiSH**,' said Dad.

Ranjit had a quizzical expression on his face. Even Steve was giving Dad a **funny** look. Nobody is as **random** as my parents when it comes to expressing annoyance.

'Sheep?' said Daniel. 'What's the problem, just shoo them away! I bet they'll run when they see the train coming.'

'It's against animal protection rules to just drive a big fat train right into a herd of sheep,' said Maryam.

'*Hmmm*, I'm sure they'll get them moving along pretty quickly,' said Dad, looking at his watch as if he didn't believe his own words.

'Are we still going to make it? Are you

worried?' I asked him.

'Worried? I'm not worried,' said Dad in a voice that got higher as he spoke.

'Then why do you sound squeaky?' said Daniel.

'I don't,' said

SQUEAKY Dad,

and then in a fake deep voice, 'I don't.'

There was another announcement:

THE LOCAL FARM HAS BEEN CONTACTED. WE SHOULD BE ON OUR WAY AS SOON AS THE SITUATION HAS BEEN TAKEN CARE OF. WE APOLOGISE FOR THE INCONVENIENCE THIS HAS CAUSED.

Dad sighed, dropping his head, 'OK, now I'm worried. We could be stuck here a while.'

Daniel ran to the train doors and started banging on them to open.

'I'll get those silly sheep off!' he said.

Dad had to go and calm him down.

'I HATE sheep!' Daniel was yelling as Dad led him back to his seat, with everyone staring.

I imagined a huge sheep-shaped helicopter coming to the rescue, safely sucking the sheep up in a cosy long tunnel and taking them home. There were so many emergency vehicles that I could dream up which would make the world a better place. Police cars and fire engines can't do everything.

Finally, the farmers cleared the sheep, with the help of another very useful dog. I decided that if I had to be near that dog too, I would probably be **OK**.

'Let's pray there are no more hiccups now,' Dad said as the train set off again.

'Yeah, do one of your prayers to *Allah*,' Charlie said to me.

My friends knew I **always** talked to Allah whenever we needed help with something.

'OK.' I smiled and then said in a quiet voice, *Oh Allah,* first of all, thank you for making me not   that afraid of dogs any more, well, at least Steve. And please make sure we can get a nice signed Angelina Kind book for Suzy. Thank you, Allah. *Ameen.*'

I saw Charlie join his bright red inky hands
together to make a prayer, too. He gave me a big

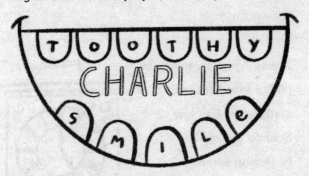

when he opened his eyes again.

CHAPTER 7

It was 7 p.m. as the train pulled into Glasgow station. We had one hour to get to the bookshop where Angelina Kind was, before her event finished. That seemed like plenty of time now that we were so close. Daniel was

super excited

We were hopeful that

OPERATION KIND

would still be a success, even after all the many hiccups we had had.

I gave Steve a quick pat as we all said
goodbye to Ranjit and dashed off the train
like we were racing against time ...
which we were!

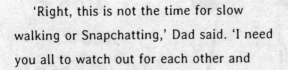

'Right, this is not the time for slow
walking or Snapchatting,' Dad said. 'I need
you all to watch out for each other and

STAY CLOSE TO ME!'

We ran through the station in a complete

frenzy,

with Dad as our guide,
looking for the exit.
   Suddenly Daniel
stopped. 'I need to

peeee!'

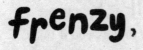

'Can you hold it?' said Dad.

'I thought I could but I can't hold it and run,' said Daniel sheepishly.

'Why didn't you go on the train?' said Maryam, sounding exactly like Mum.

'I didn't need to go then!'

'Think about something else?' suggested Charlie.

'All I can think about is that I'm bursting!' The toilets in a SUPER big station aren't as easy to find as you'd think, especially when you're all panicky and rushing about and trying not to lose each other. 'I never thought I would ever be this happy to see toilets,' said Daniel, when we finally found them.

Argggghhghhghgh,

he spoke too soon. You had to pay 50p to use them and none of us had any coins.

'NOOOOOO!' said Daniel.

'I'm going to wet myself!'

'No, you're not. Just sit down,' said Dad. 'I'm going to have to get some cash out and then I'll have to quickly buy something from a shop to get change.'

Poor Daniel. I felt really sorry for him. He looked *super* uncomfortable. I knew that the only reason Operation Kind was out of Daniel's mind for the moment was because he could only think about

OPERATION RELIEF

– you will NEVER feel more relieved in your life than when you're bursting for the loo and then get to go. Except maybe if you have a really, really terrible dream and wake up and realise it wasn't real. That and the pee thing are the most *phew, what a relieeeeeeef* feelings EVER!

Seeing Daniel's face, I said, 'I need to go, too.'

And then Charlie said, 'Me too.'

We were always sticking together. I liked that A LOT.

Luckily, there was a cash machine nearby, but then Dad got stuck in a queue for aaaages at a shop to get change.

It was 7:25 p.m. when we inserted our 50p

coins in the slots and went into the stinky toilets.

And then something happened which meant that Daniel was going to have to face one of his biggest fears if he wanted to complete

OPERATION KIND.

CHAPTER 8

Daniel came out of the cubicle after finally relieving himself, saw me and *Smiled* and said, 'I can't believe we're going to meet Angelina Kind.' As he opened the tap to wash his hands the tap came off in his hands, sending water squirting right on to his jeans.

It looked as if he had wet himself. I couldn't believe that happened after Daniel had managed to keep it in **THE WHOLE TIME** we tried to get to the toilets.

Daniel went red, matching Charlie's hands and chin. 'I can't go to Angelina Kind like this! It's like meeting

BATMAN

with your underpants on your head!'

I just stared, as Charlie walked over to wash his hands.

'What? Daniel? Did you wet yourself?' he asked.

'No! No! No! No!'

'Are you sure?'

I couldn't help but giggle. But as I was an eyewitness it was very important that I speak up.

'It's water from the tap.

I SAW it happen,'

I told Charlie. Then I said to Daniel, 'Maybe it will dry by the time we get to her?'

'I don't think so – jeans take ages to dry!' Daniel looked like he was in COMPLETE agony. 'What am I going to do? I can't go like this. Angelina Kind will think I wet myself. And everyone else will too. I have to walk in PUBLIC like this!'

Because of an incident that happened when Daniel and I first met, it's his worst nightmare for people to think that he is someone who wets his pants. I won't tell you what it was (although you might already know) because Daniel is my friend now and I will keep his **SECRETS** for ever.

'We could stand in front of you when we meet her?'

'No!'

'Then we'll have to go in and get the book signed while you wait outside,' I said.

'Fine,' said Daniel, shoulders drooping.

We walked out of the toilets to where Dad and Maryam were **WAITING.**

'Did you wet your pants, Daniel?' said Maryam right away.

I did my duty as the sole eyewitness and told them everything as we ran to the exit.

We had planned to get a taxi, but the road outside the station was filled with traffic at a complete standstill.

Dad's face d r o p p e d as he looked at the map on his phone. 'We're going to have to walk, but there's a good chance we'll be late. Are you ready to walk faster than you've ever walked before?'

Daniel put his hand on my dad's arm. 'Mr Omar's

dad, we haven't come this far to be defeated by a little bit of walking! Omar and Charlie have faced their biggest FEARS to be here and ... well ... I'm going to face mine too. I'm going to meet Angelina Kind and get the book signed myself,' he said, then paused before shouting at the top of his voice:

'WITH THESE TROUSERS ON!'

We all whooped and cheered, while everyone near us stared like we were ALieNs.

We started jogging down the street, following the map towards the bookshop. I imagined my feet had hundreds more tiny feet attached to them, to make me go a hundred times faster. After about

five minutes, Dad suddenly yelped as he went flying face first **on to the pavement!**

'**AAARRGH ⊗UCH!**'

he yelped.

'For the love of fish fingers. I've twisted my ankle on a loose paving stone. I'm not sure if I can walk on it.'

We all looked at each other. We were SO CLOSE. I thought I might burst into tears, but Maryam took charge right away: 'Daniel and Charlie, you're going to have to lift a leg each. Omar, you and I will lift under Dad's shoulders. We'll make it, even if we have to carry him *all the way!*'

'YES SIR, MARYAM SIR!'

Daniel shouted like he was in the army.

Dad started to protest, but we were already lifting him up – and I don't know whether there was an angel helping us, but I barely noticed how HEAVY he was at all.

At 8:05 p.m. we could see the bookshop up ahead.

It was like seeing water after walking through the desert for days.

We carried Dad **AS FAST AS HUMANLY POSSIBLE** until, panting, we made it to the door and were able to put him down. Daniel rushed into the shop, with the rest of us following close behind.

'Where is she?' Daniel asked desperately.

But there were only two people in the bookshop. And neither of them was Angelina Kind.

CHAPTER 9

'We're so sorry, she had a train to catch so wrapped up promptly at 8 o'clock,' explained one shop assistant.

I felt like I had been hit in the chest by

A RHINO.

Daniel must have felt even worse. He let himself fall to the floor and put his face in the carpet, just like he had done that morning in my room, except now he was sobbing.

'Why didn't it work? You made me one of your prayers.'

I didn't know why. It usually does work. But Mum always tells me that when I pray for something, I have to trust that *Allah* will sort it out in a way that He knows is best for me, even if it means not getting what I asked for. I still couldn't believe it though – I really thought after all those obstacles, it would be a happy ending and we would get to the bookshop in time to meet Angelina Kind.

Dad was sitting down next to Daniel, just patting his back. He wasn't saying anything. He was letting Daniel have a moment.

Maryam took her phone out to record.

'You can't record him crying,' **hissed** Charlie.

'Yes, I can,' said Maryam. 'It's all part of the story.'

Dad ordered Maryam to put the phone away and **stop being so insensitive.**

She did put it away, but her face told me she had already caught the action she needed.

The two bookstore owners were very sorry for Daniel – and all of us, really. They made us hot chocolates to cheer us up. While Charlie explained to the shop owners why his hands

and chin were bright red, Dad had a little chat with Daniel to try and calm him down again.

'Sometimes things don't work out the way we plan them, Daniel. But I truly believe that everything happens for a reason.

I am very
                proud of you

for doing everything that you did to get here. Suzy is going to love hearing this story of

✦ OPERATION ♥KIND.

It will make her extremely happy knowing she has a big brother who did all that for her.'

Daniel sat up and wiped his dripping snot on the back of his hand.

'I guess that's true,' he managed, sniffing the rest of the snot back up his nose as he spoke. 'It will be a cool story to tell her.'

'Absolutely,' said Dad.

And then, cheeeeeesy as it might sound, we had a group **hug**. Daniel, Charlie, Maryam, Dad and me. Well, Maryam jumped out of it for a second to take a picture.

'Maryam!' we all said, and we laughed and hugged away our sadness.

Dad had found a hotel for us to stay the night in since it was such a

LOOOOONG

journey. When we got there, we ordered room service pizzas and milkshakes, ate, brushed our teeth and fell asleep as soon as our heads hit the pillows.

In the morning we would take the train
back to London.

CHAPTER 10

Do you know the weirdest thing? Not one

teeny tiny thing

went wrong on our journey home. Dad's ankle felt completely BETTER, and the train ride was so smooth, I imagined there must have been angels keeping trouble out of our way, including funny ticket ladies and animals on the tracks.

Poor Daniel was dropped off home without a signed Angelina Kind book. But he was being very brave about it.

'Maybe I'll write Suzy a book called

✦OPERATION KIND✦,'

he had said in the car. 'Will you guys draw the pictures?'

We felt good that at least Daniel had that.

He didn't want anyone to tell Suzy the story until we made the book so, a couple of days later, we got together at my house again.

'THAT LOOKS LiKE A RECTANGLE WiTH LEGS AND FLUFF. MAKE iT MORE SHEEPY,'

Daniel said. He was really taking

CHARGE.

'OK.' Charlie laughed.

'How do you spell "obstacles"?' Daniel said, as his phone rang.

It was Daniel's mum. She said she had just spoken to my mum and that she was going to drive us all to the hospital to see Suzy.

'But the book isn't finished yet!' Daniel protested.

'Don't worry about it, dear, just come.'

Then my mum walked in and said, 'Get in the PEANUT quickly.'

She was acting **SUPER, SUPER** weird.

'What on earth is going on?' Charlie said as we stuck our feet in our trainers.

'Who knows?' Daniel shrugged.

'Just **ADULTS being ADULTS,**

I guess,' I said.

We parked up at the hospital and walked into the ward where Suzy was. Her room's blinds were drawn, so we couldn't see in.

The mysterious ways of our parents were driving us **nuts**. We tried to peep through the blinds, but we couldn't see a thing.

Then Daniel's dad opened the door. We saw a bright,

SUPER
excited~looking
Suzy.

And right next to her bed, was stood none other than ... ANGELINA KIND!!!!

For some reason, the first thing Daniel did was look down at his jeans.

(Haha, actually we know the reason!) But this time, Daniel's trousers were dry. Unlike his eyes, because the shock and joy sent happy tears rolling down his cheeks as Angelina Kind gave him a big hug.

How had Angelina Kind ended up right next to us, after our mission

FAILED?

We had a **THOUSAND QUESTIONS** and she very kindly explained it all to us.

When she had settled down on her train journey (TO LONDON!) she checked her social media and saw she'd been tagged in all of Maryam's posts recording

OPERATION KIND

She said she was moved to tears so she rang the bookshop and asked if they knew how to get in touch with us. Apparently

SUPER DAD

had thought to leave his contact details so they arranged it all.

Suzy got a lovely long message in her book and a special video of the two of them together.

It was

SUPER
Awesome.

We talked excitedly all the way home. And we kept talking about it for weeks!

We would say things like, 'Remember when Angelina Kind said we were brave?', even though it had only happened a few days ago. And we smiled so much our cheeks hurt.

'**Hey!** your prayer did work! It just
worked in a different way than we thought,'
said Daniel.

'**YEP!**

Allah is SO cool!'

I giggled.

Daniel finished creating his book, with its
unexpected happy ending.

OPERATION KIND
hAd turned out
to bE our
BEST
mission yet.

On your bookmarks, get set, read!

Well hello there! We are

Overjoyed that you have joined our celebration of

Reading books and sharing stories, because we

Love bringing books to you.

Did you know, we are a charity dedicated to celebrating the

Brilliance of reading for pleasure for everyone, everywhere?

Our mission is to help you discover brand new stories and

Open your mind to exciting worlds and characters, from

Kings and queens to wizards and pirates to animals and adventurers and so many more. We couldn't

Do it without all the amazing authors and illustrators, booksellers and bookshops, publishers, schools and libraries out there –

And most importantly, we couldn't do it all without . . .

You!

WORLD BOOK DAY

Share a story

From breakfast to bedtime, there's always time to discover and share stories together. You can . . .

1 Take a trip to your local bookshop

Brimming with brilliant books and helpful booksellers to share awesome reading recommendations, you can also enjoy booky events with your favourite authors and illustrators.

Find your local bookshop:
booksellers.org.uk/bookshopsearch

2 Join your local library

That wonderful place where the hugest selection of books you could ever want to read awaits – and you can borrow them for FREE! Plus expert advice and fantastic free family reading events.

Find your local library:
gov.uk/local-library-services/

3 Check out the World Book Day website

Looking for reading tips, advice and inspiration? There is so much to discover at **worldbookday.com**, packed with fun activities, audiobooks, videos, competitions and all the latest book news galore.

Changing lives through a love of books and shared reading.
World Book Day is a registered charity funded by publishers and booksellers in the UK & Ireland.

SPONSORED BY
NATIONAL BOOK tokens

ILLUSTRATION Rob Biddulph

**Read on for a sneak peek of another
AMAZING book you might like …**

CHAPTER 1

I AM SO ANGRY I THINK MY BUM MIGHT
FALL OFF!!!!

Mr Nibbles was mine!!! Mine!!! Not stupid
William U's!!!! Mine!!!!

I think I should draw a pie chart that proves
how much I want Mr Nibbles:

Things I Really Want

3% all the plastic out of the ocean

11% Jakub to find his job

32% a UniMingo changey sequin jumper

100000000000000000% Mr Nibbles

And I don't even care that this pie chart doesn't
actually add up to a hundred per cent like pie charts
actually should. *(Which I'd normally really care about,
by the way, because that's how pie charts work and
that's why I'm on The Purple Table in Maths, which
we all know is the best one, but we have to pretend
that all the Maths tables are the same, even though The*

Green Table still haven't learned their three times table and probably think a pie chart is a menu in a cafe.) THAT'S how much I WANT MR NIBBLES!!

(By the way, I really want Mr Nibbles.)

Let me explain something:

Mr Nibbles is Rainbow Class's pet hamster and everyone at St Lidwina's Primary School loves him *(except for Vashti because she says it's important to be an individual, which is why she never brushes her hair).* Every week, everyone really wants to get the most Positivity Points so they can be Star of the Week and look after Mr Nibbles for the weekend.

I REALLY wanted Mr Nibbles to come home with me this weekend, so I have been EXTRA SUPER MEGA GOOD.

To get the most Positivity Points, I have:

• Sharpened all the pencils at playtime *(even though Darcy had the new UniMingo hairbrush and she said it was my turn to try it at playtime after Milly and Roshin, but only if Milly didn't have nits any more like she did at Parva's hair-braiding party and we all got them and school had to send A Letter Home).*

• Said thank you *all* the time *(even when I didn't mean it, like when the dinner ladies put broccoli on my plate, because the only place broccoli should EVER be put is in vegetable prison).*

• Learned my eight times tables backwards *(although I wanted to do that because Maths is my favourite and I'm really good at it, which is why I'm on* The Purple Table).

• Helped to clean up the dinner hall after lunchtime *(even though it looked like the bottom of the monkey enclosure at a wildlife park after the monkeys had a party and then had to leave calmly and quietly for a fire alarm).*

This was what the top of the Positivity Chart looked like when I got to school this morning:

Scarlett: 29

Matthew: 27

Maisie: 25

William U: 24

Vashti: 23

(I was a bit worried when Vashti got four Positivity Points for actually brushing her hair for the school

photo, but she broke Darcy's UniMingo hairbrush doing it, so that was the end of that.)

Mr Nibbles was mine. I was all ready for him and even made a special Mr Nibbles area in my bedroom with:

• A bed.

• A bath.

• An obstacle course (*I don't want him to get bored*).

• A book (*in case he wakes up in the night with bad dreams and can't sleep*).

• A night light (*I don't want him to be scared and wake up with bad dreams*).

• A teddy (*which I took out because it was bigger than him and I thought it might give him bad dreams despite the night light and then he might not like the book to get back to sleep*).

I was SUPER EXCITED because I've never had Mr Nibbles before …

And then this afternoon I went to the Positivity Chart to see:

William U: 32

Scarlett: 29

Matthew: 27

Vashti: 26

(She borrowed someone else's brush for the school photo.)

Maisie: 25

… and William U standing smugly next to Mr Nibbles's cage.

'WHAT?????!!!!' I shouted. 'EIGHT POSITIVITY POINTS? HOW DID YOU GET EIGHT POSITIVITY POINTS! When the dinner ladies accidentally set the fish fingers on fire, the firefighters who saved the school didn't get EIGHT POSITIVITY POINTS! How did you …?'

But then I followed his smug look in the direction of Mrs Underwood. Our teaching assistant.

And also William U's mum.

Let me explain something:

William U *always* gets Mr Nibbles. William U *always* gets everything he wants. And if William U doesn't get what he wants, William U's mum *always* gets it for him.

William U *always* gets loads of Positivity Points and has *never* been stuck at the bottom of the chart, even though he should live at the bottom because he's super mean to everyone, but especially me because:

1) I'm much better than William U at Maths and he likes to be best at everything.

2) The one time William U came to my house for a playdate, he tried to pull the head off my UniMingo slippers and I told on him and my mum told his mum and although he never gets in trouble with his mum, he's never forgiven me for telling on him.

3) William U probably can't think of a third thing because I'm better than him at Maths.

(By the way, William U isn't to be confused with William D who can name all the dinosaurs and once ate a snail, even though William D WASN'T in France and the snail WAS in his garden.)

William U's mum used to work as a lawyer with my Aunty Rosa *(which is how bogie-head William*

U got invited to her engagement party, so I've got to see him tonight as WELL as all day at school). Aunty Rosa told me that William U's mum used to get upset about people not getting paid enough, and people being treated unfairly, and people's human rights not being respected.

But then William U's mum gave up being a lawyer and had William U. So now William U's mum mainly gets upset about What Upset William. And if William U wants Mr Nibbles, his mum will do anything to make sure that happens.

WILL SCARLETT MANAGE TO STOP
WILLIAM U FROM BEING SO SNEAKY,
BRING MR NIBBLES HOME AND KEEP
HER ANGER UNDER CONTROL?

SOUNDS ALMOST IMPOSSIBLE TO US!
FIND OUT MORE IN
*THE EXPLODING LIFE
OF SCARLETT FIFE,*
IN BOOKSHOPS FROM MAY 2021